QUIET

QUIET

PETER PARNALL

MORROW JUNIOR BOOKS / NEW YORK

Printed in the United States of America.   1 2 3 4 5 6 7 8 9 10
Library of Congress Cataloging-in-Publication Data
Parnall, Peter.   Quiet / Peter Parnall.   p.   cm.
    Summary: A child lies quietly on the ground and waits for the animals to come near.
    ISBN 0-688-08204-1.—ISBN 0-688-08205-X (lib. bdg.)
    [1. Animals—Fiction. 2. Quietude—Fiction. 3. Nature—Fiction.] I. Title.
    PZ7.P243Qu   1989   [E]—dc19   89-2847   CIP   AC

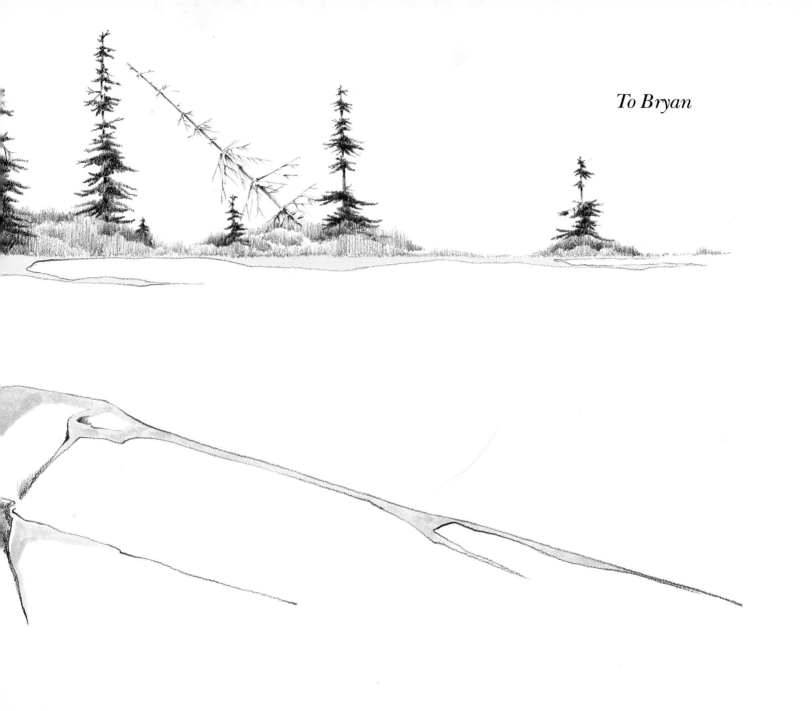

To Bryan

Quietly I lie on the grass.

QUIET.... Small breaths, no rustling cloth,
no twitches or blinks.
No sound . . .

And Raven watches. He watches Chipmunk watching me.
They don't know what I am when I'm stretched out flat.

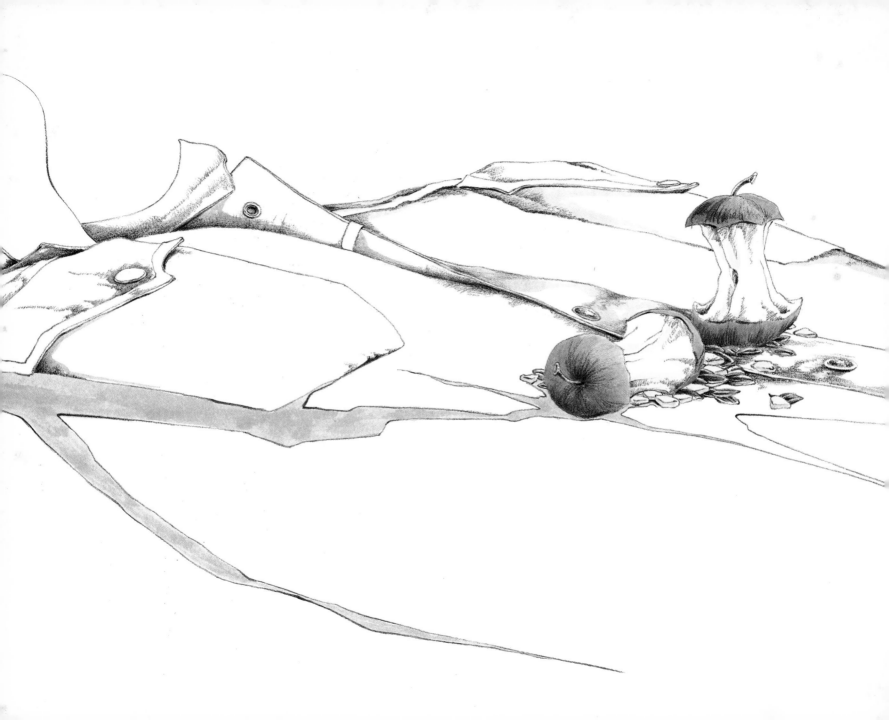

Chipmunk comes when he sees me there,
a quiet, wrinkled thing under a pile of seeds and
apple cores.

Raven, too, on straining wings comes close enough . . .

to mess my hair.

Clouds tumble by from over the hill and Grizzly Bears
come to help me wait.

I see Bumblebees drone on their daily rounds,

closely!

Now— QUIET —let me meet a Chickadee.

I lie on the lawn with the seeds on my chest,
waiting for one to come by for a treat.

As I wait, I hear Mouse rustle under leaves by my head . . .

And hear whispers in the pines where Raven sits . . .
whispers from wind that blew in from the sea,

From the sea where Vikings roamed near Maine
and maybe met a bird on an outstretched hand . . .

Like this one, here, on my chest! QUIET . . . . No sound.

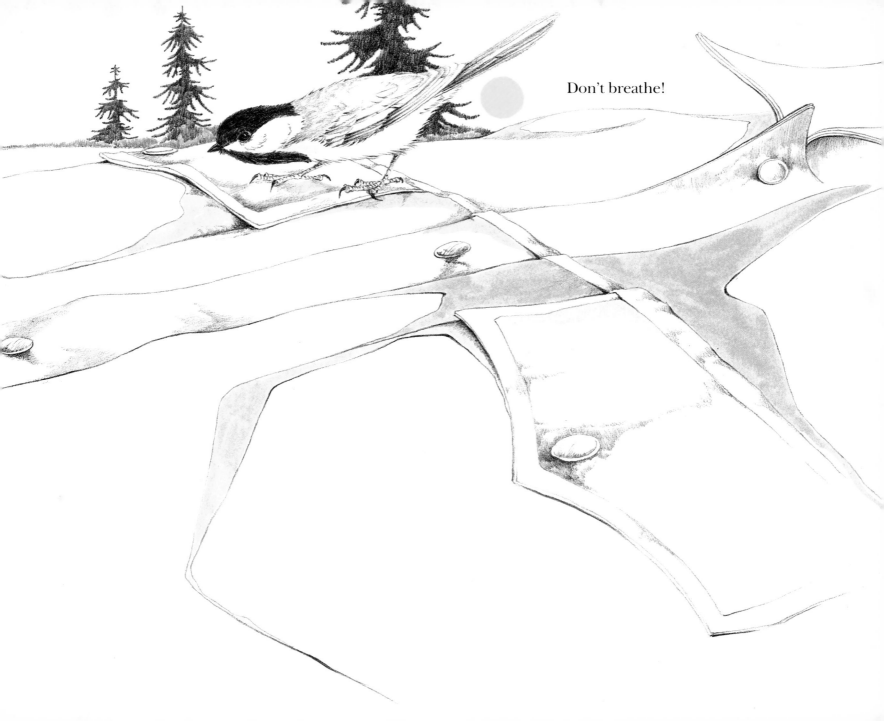

Don't breathe!

The only thing they can hear as they dart in for a seed
is my heart saying, "Stay. Stay, little birds. Stay with
me, Chickadees."

Raven watches.
He watches Chipmunk and me,
and Chickadees.

QUIETLY.